Romping

Romping Through Ulysses

First edition 2012
UCLA edition 2013
Second edition 2013
Published by At it Again!
Printed in Dublin by Johnston Print & Design

Text and Illustrations by Niall Laverty, Maite López-Schröder,
James Moore and Jessica Peel-Yates. They assert their moral
rights to be identified as the authors of this work.

ISBN 978-0-9576559-1-1

www.atitagain.ie

Contents

James Joyce 1882 - 1941

James Joyce was the Andy Warhol of his day. He was a self-declared genius and an outrageous self-publicist. When asked *"Whom do you consider the greatest writers in English today?"* he replied *"Aside from myself? I don't know."*

He dabbled in poetry, short stories, plays, novels, singing, and selling Irish tweed. He also opened the first cinema in Dublin. When writing he liked to have a lazy morning, an industrious afternoon and a chaotic evening. Beneath his erratic exterior, he was a very disciplined man.

A cunning linguist, he eloped to Europe with his lover, Nora Barnacle, to live a life of artistic exile. They had two children and secretly married years later. Joyce joked that he named his children *"Sense and Sensibility"* after Jane Austen's book.

As a student he was considered the bad boy of Dublin. Even today Dubliners love to hate him. He sponged off friends and family until he found patrons to fund his creativity and unconventional lifestyle. Laughing at his reputation, he called himself *"an international eyesore"* having had eleven eye operations in eight years.

Joyce loved to create legends and rumours about himself. Did he drink with Lenin in Zurich? Was it true that Picasso refused to paint his portrait? Did he and Samuel Beckett have silent conversations? Was *"memento homo"* tattooed across his bum?

Ulysses

Ulysses loosely mirrors Homer's *Odyssey*. Like a soap opera, it deals with sex, drink, adultery, life and death. And of course, religion and guilt. Joyce adopted lots of different writing styles to create *Ulysses*, making the book a carnival of language and a celebration of existence. You'll discover hilarity and grief, quirks and contradictions, the weird and surreal.

The main characters are Leopold Bloom and Stephen Dedalus. As each journeys across Dublin, they experience all of life in one day. Autobiography and fiction merge, with Joyce basing his characters on real people. Because of his love/hate relationship with the city, Dublin plays a central role.

It took Joyce over 10 years to write *Ulysses*. Considered indecent by most publishers, an American in Paris finally agreed to print it in 1922. To critics who found *Ulysses* obscene and unreadable, Joyce said *"if Ulysses isn't fit to read, then life isn't fit to live."* Today it is regarded as one of the greatest novels in the English language.

The story of *Ulysses* is set on the 16th June 1904. This day has become known as Bloomsday. Named after the book's anti-hero, Leopold Bloom, it is celebrated every year around the world.

How to use your Manual

Use the manual to create your own romp through *Ulysses*. It's also a handy guide for exploring Dublin. Dip into it as an introduction if you are reading *Ulysses* for the first time or if you are at it again!

With this manual you can become part of the story. Events from *Ulysses* unfold hour by hour from morning to night-time. You will find out what's happening in the story, get ideas of what to do and places to visit. Arm yourself with a quote or two and pick up some insider titbits.

> 🍂 For a city centre walk, use the route opposite as a guide.

> 🍂 If you have more time, *Ulysses The Map* in the centre of the manual will help you plan your adventure.

To really immerse yourself in the story, why not dress up and create your own characters? This manual will give you some ideas.

Learn to love Dublin and stop fearing *Ulysses*!

Romping through Dublin

ULYSSES THE WALK

| | James Joyce Centre
Calypso |
| A | |

| B | The Prick with the Stick
Aeolus |

| C | Irish Independent Building
Aeolus |

| D | St. Andrew's Church
Lotus Eaters |

| E | Sweny's Chemist
Lotus Eaters |

| F | National Library
Scylla & Charybdis |

| G | National Museum
Lestrygonians |

| H | Davy Byrne's Pub
Lestrygonians |

| I | Merchant's Arch
Wandering Rocks |

| J | Ormond Quay
Sirens |

| K | Little Britain Street
Cyclops |

Ulysses The Walk
Route (3.5km approx.)

4

Meet the Cast

Main Characters

Leopold Bloom – a practical but whimsical jack of all trades. A fair-weather Jew searching for a son. A bit of a bore. A saviour with an eye for the ladies. He sweats through the day in his black funeral suit and bowler hat.

Stephen Dedalus – a youthful poet, idealist and restless intellectual. He loves his floppy bohemian Latin Quarter hat and his walking stick. His friends think they are a bit naff. Called back from Paris by the death of his mother, he swans around Dublin getting drunk.

Molly Bloom – concert soprano who enjoys racy novels, breakfast and other activities in bed. She is in and out of her nightie for most of the day. Born in Gibraltar, she has a reputation for being hot-blooded.

Blazes Boylan – man about town, concert tour manager and afternoon lover of Molly Bloom. He flirts his way around Dublin in a straw hat, sky-blue bow tie and a red flower in his buttonhole.

Malachi "Buck" Mulligan – Stephen's flamboyant, sharp-tongued flatmate. A bit of a user. He has a thing for yellow dressing gowns and waistcoats, except when he is dressed in his medical student whites.

Supporting Characters

Paddy Dignam – like many characters in the book, he's ruined by drink. So ruined, it killed him. For a dead man, he's got a large role! Ghost-like, he pops up throughout the story.

Lamppost Farrell – a real Dublin eccentric who fell into a barrel of Guinness. Wearing a skullcap and twirling an umbrella, he haunts the streets dancing on the outside of lampposts.

HELY'S Men – five sandwich board men for a Dublin stationery company. They walk the streets in white smocks and tall white hats each bearing a red letter spelling out the company name.

Mina Kennedy and Lydia Douce – the delicious sirens, tempting gentlemen with song and thigh. One has gold hair, the other bronze. They keep their customers happy by flashing their garters.

The Citizen – one-eyed bully with a scraggly hound called Garryowen. Spouts forth on every topic under the sun and roundly abuses Bloom. Imagine him with an eye patch, wielding a biscuit tin.

Gerty MacDowell – the young romantic on the beach, who causes a middle-aged man to overheat. She thinks she is the height of fashion dressed in blue from head to toe including blue undies for luck!

Bella Cohen – society hostess and brothel owner. A resident of Nighttown, she wears an ivory gown, is draped in jewellery and brandishes a black fan. She briefly undergoes a sex change and dominates Bloom.

W. B. Murphy – a shifty seaman full of tall stories who likes to hang out in late night joints. Wearing his sailor's uniform and smothered in tattoos, he swigs from his hip flask.

How to Dress the Character

Ulysses is set in the Edwardian era. Here are some ideas for dressing up.
Or check out Meet the Cast for more adventurous getups.

Ladies

The *S-bend* and the *mono-bosom* reigned supreme. Your boobs were sticking out
in front, and your padded arse stuck out behind. All held in place by a vicious
contraption called a corset. So as not to fall over in these postures, some ladies
resorted to the use of parasols and canes.

To create an easy Edwardian look dig out a long skirt, coupled with a high-
collared blouse. Wind a big belt or scarf around your waist and drape a shawl
across your shoulders. Or pimp an old evening gown. Accessories such as a hat
and gloves were a must for the society lady.

This was the era of wigs, hairpieces, and padding. For the *Pompadour* style your
hair sits in a big cloud on your head. You can top it off with a bun. Go mad with
back combing and hair spray. If you have short hair, try a hat or maid's cap.
Make-up was subtle, but slap it on if you are feeling naughty!

How to Dress the Character

Gents

In all things Edwardian, the Prince of Wales was the ultimate trendsetter. Most common was the three-piece suit with a coat, a waistcoat and upturned trousers. Shirts had stiff, high collars, making turning your head a challenge. The Edwardian gentleman sported an array of accessories from bow ties, gloves, walking sticks with secret compartments, to pocket watches. Most importantly, the man of the world wouldn't dream of leaving home without a hat!

To create an easy Edwardian look, pull on a pair of trousers, iron a shirt and adorn your neck with a bow tie or handkerchief. Put on a jacket, blazer or waistcoat, or just hold your trousers up with a pair of braces. A hat will finish off the costume. Make it a bowler, a straw hat or a cap. Accessorise with a macintosh, spectacles, walking stick or a flower in your lapel.

Hair was short and neat, parted in the middle or at the side, and slicked back with pomade. Beards were out and pampered moustaches were in.

Part 1

Morning

*"Somewhere in the East. Early morning: set off at dawn,
travel round in front of the sun steal a day's march on him.
Keep it up for ever never grow a day older technically."*

8 am

Telemachus - The one with the shave and the swim

Location No 1: Stephen Dedalus at the Martello Tower in Sandycove

What's the story?

Stately, plump Buck Mulligan, Stephen Dedalus and their English tower mate arise to greet the day with their morning rituals. Mulligan shaves on top of the tower imitating a priest at mass with his shaving bowl. He mocks Stephen for not kneeling down to pray at his mother's death bed. He jokes that the shock killed her. They share breakfast before Mulligan takes a dip in the *scrotumtightening* sea. Stephen, irritated by the others, leaves for work vowing never to return. Ironically, he is the one paying the rent.

"Isn't the sea what Algy calls it: a grey sweet mother?"

Why don't you...?

- Visit the James Joyce Tower and Museum in Sandycove.

- Shave, but keep moustache or whiskers for the Edwardian look.

- Share a breakfast of eggs, tea, toast, honey, and sugar.

- Enjoy a swim in the Forty Foot bathing place or dip your toe in some other watering hole.

He said, she said...

"The bard's noserag. A new colour for our Irish poets: snotgreen. You can almost taste it, can't you?" - Buck Mulligan.

Titbit

Traditionally, the Forty Foot was an all-male stronghold for nude bathing. Then, in the 1970s a female invasion took place. It became known as the *"Attack of the Forty Foot Women!"*

8 am

Calypso - The one with the shit

Location No 2: Leopold Bloom at No 7 Eccles Street

What's the story?

Leopold Bloom potters around the kitchen, preparing breakfast. He chats to the cat. *Mkgnao!* He pops to the butcher's for a kidney, where he ogles the vigorous hips of a local girl. Back home, Bloom takes tea up to Molly, who is still in bed. Molly tells Bloom that Blazes Boylan is coming for a rendez-vous at 4pm. Then she asks him to pick up a racy novel while he's out. Armed with a paper he heads for the outhouse.

"Quietly he read, restraining himself, the first column and, yielding but resisting, began the second."

Why don't you...?

- Fry yourself a kidney for breakfast.

- Visit the James Joyce Centre on North Great George's Street to see the original door of No 7 Eccles Street.

- Read the paper on the bog.

He said, she said...

"Good puzzle would be cross Dublin without passing a pub" - Leopold Bloom.

Titbit

Leopold Bloom's birthplace is 52 Clanbrassil Street, which would have been part of Dublin's Jewish quarter. There is a plaque to commemorate this fictitious fact.

9.45 am
Nestor – The one with the rant

Location No 3: Stephen at Dalkey School on Dalkey Avenue

What's the story?

Stephen is a school teacher. He's supposed to be teaching history, but his students are more interested in ghost stories, riddles and hockey. Futility. He helps a boy with his sums. It's payday! Mr Deasy, the anti-Semitic headmaster, asks Stephen to use his press connections to get a letter published. He rants about foot and mouth disease, women and the state of the nation while Stephen bows and smiles.

"Thought is the thought of thought."

Why don't you...?

- Write a letter of complaint to the editor of an Irish newspaper.

- Tell a ghost story.

- Rant about the state of the nation to anyone who will listen.

He said, she said...

"History is a nightmare from which I am trying to awake" - Stephen Dedalus.

Titbit

Joyce started school at the age of *"half past six."* He went to Belvedere College for a while. You'll find it at the top of North Great George's Street.

9.45 am
Lotus Eaters - The one with the soap

Location No 4: Bloom around Westland Row and Lincoln Place

What's the story?

Bloom collects a letter from Martha, his secret pen friend, at a post office. A passing acquaintance asks about Molly's upcoming concert tour, alluding to her affair with Blazes Boylan. Bloom pops into St Andrew's Church for some religious stupefaction. Floating into Sweny's Chemist, he buys some lemon soap. A misunderstanding over a discarded newspaper starts a rumour that Bloom has bet on a 20-1 horse named Throwaway. He ogles women and thinks about taking a Turkish bath.

"The limp father of thousands,

a languid floating flower."

Why don't you...?

- Visit Sweny's Chemist on Lincoln Place where you can buy lemon soap.

- Enter St. Andrew's Church on Westland Row from the rear.

- Wink at someone you find attractive.

- Place a bet on a horse with long odds.

He said, she said...

"The priest went along by them, holding the thing in his hands. The priest bent down to put it into her mouth, murmuring all the time" - Bloom.

Titbit

Turkish baths were popular in Dublin at the turn of the 20th century. But they were not just for people. The one on Lincoln Place had a back entrance where horses and other animals could avail of a sauna and massage.

11 am
Proteus – The one in eternity

Location No 5: Stephen on Sandymount Strand

What's the story?

Stephen, the dreamer, takes a stroll on Sandymount Strand. He imagines he's blind and taps along with his cane. He thinks about his writing career and his dead mother. He recalls vivid memories of his recent stay in Paris. Imagination enfolds him, as nearly does the turning tide. Across the expansive sand a dog bounds. Our bard has a stab at writing a poem and picks his nose.

Oi!

"I am getting on nicely in the dark."

Why don't you...?

- Walk out into eternity on Sandymount Strand.
- Close your eyes and imagine you are blind - identify sounds around you.
- Write something in the sand.
- Check out what Bloom gets up to later on the Strand in *Nausicaa*.

He said, she said...

"Ineluctable modality of the visible: at least that if no more, thought through my eyes. Signatures of all things I am here to read, seaspawn and seawrack, the nearing tide, that rusty boot" - Stephen.

Titbit

In 2013, the Irish Central Bank issued a commemorative €10 Joyce coin. It's funny THAT they got THAT quote wrong.

11 am

Hades - The one with the funeral

Location No 6: Bloom at Glasnevin Cemetery

What's the story?

Paddy Dignam's funeral carriage clip-clops across Dublin from Sandymount to Glasnevin Cemetery. Thought and talk meander from life to death. For the cemetery caretaker, it's all in a day's work. *Shovelling them under by the cartload doublequick.* Twelve mourners and a mysterious man in a macintosh pray at the graveside. Bloom thinks about all the decomposing bodies. What's that? A fat grey rat.

*"Paddy Dignam shot out...
Mouth fallen open.
Asking what's up now."*

Why don't you...?

- Visit Glasnevin Cemetery.

- Take a carriage ride around Dublin.

- Search out the Gravediggers Pub where the diggers were served their pints through a hole in the wall.

He said, she said...

"As you are now so once were we" - Bloom.

Titbit

In Parisian café society, Joyce was known for his wild drunken dancing. Dance the Glasnevin Shuffle in his honour.

Glasnevin Shuffle

Take a drink to the left and then a drink to the right.
Do the Glasnevin Shuffle, cos you've been boozing all your life.
Stagger forward like a zombie, then shuffle back to your grave.
Add old school wacko jacko, you're doing the Paddy Dignam rave!

Part 2

Afternoon

"The hungry famished gull
Flaps o'er the waters dull."

12.15 pm

Aeolus – The one with the headlines

Location No 7: Bloom and Stephen at the Freeman's Journal on Middle Abbey Street

What's the story?

Bloom goes into the newspaper office to discuss the placement of an ad. There is a lot of hot air talked. He is blown off course by the rudeness of the editor. Stephen comes in to get Mr. Deasy's letter published. On the way to the pub, Stephen tells a parable. It's about two Dublin spinsters spitting plum stones from the top of Nelson's Pillar.

Freeman's Journal

RETURN OF BLOOM

K.M.A.

"Will you tell him he can kiss my arse?"

"K.M.R.I.A."

Why don't you...?

- Pose with *The Prick with the Stick* on Earl Street North near the Spire.

- Find the old Irish Independent building on Middle Abbey Street.

- Visit the National Print Museum on Haddington Road to see the old printing machines.

He said, she said...

"Shite and onions!" - Stephen's dad.

Titbit

Nelson's Pillar used to stand where the Spire is now. It was blown up in 1966 by the Irish Republican Army. See the original head from the pillar in the library at 138 – 144 Pearse Street.

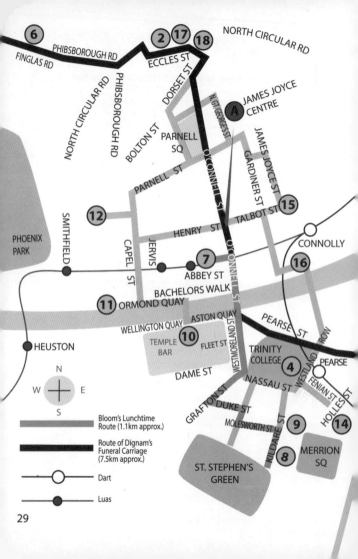

29

Romping through Dublin

ULYSSES THE MAP

1. Martello Tower, Sandycove (Telemachus)
2. No 7 Eccles Street (Calypso)
3. Dalkey School, Dalkey Avenue (Nestor)
4. Sweny's Chemist, Lincoln Place (Lotus Eaters)
5. Sandymount Strand (Proteus)
6. Glasnevin Cemetery (Hades)
7. Middle Abbey Street (Aeolus)
8. National Museum (Lestrygonians)
9. National Library (Scylla and Charybdis)
10. Merchants Arch (Wandering Rocks)
11. Ormond Hotel Bar (Sirens)
12. Little Britain Street (Cyclops)
13. Sandymount Strand (Nausicaa)
14. Holles Street (Oxen of the Sun)
15. James Joyce Street, Monto (Circe)
16. Butt Bridge, Custom House Quay (Eumaeus)
17. No 7 Eccles Street (Ithaca)
18. No 7 Eccles Street (Penelope)

RINGSEND RD

IRISHTOWN RD

BEACH RD

SANDYCOVE (1)

(13) (5)

DALKEY

NEWBRIDGE AVENUE

SANDYMOUNT RD

(3)

LANDSDOWNE

AVE

SANDYMOUNT

Please Note: Map not to Scale

1.10 pm

Lestrygonians – The one with the arseholes

Location No 8: Bloom from Middle Abbey Street to the National Museum

What's the story?

Bloom goes in search of lunch. On the way, he spots Lamppost Farrell, the HELY'S men with their tall white hats, and bumps into an old flame. He is disgusted by the greedy pigs in one restaurant. Ending up in Davy Byrne's he decides on gorgonzola cheese and Burgundy wine. He remembers being intimate with Molly on Howth Head for the first time. Trying to avoid Blazes Boylan, he ducks into the National Museum to see if Greek statues have anuses.

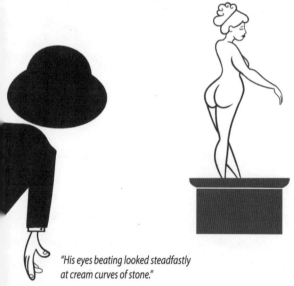

"His eyes beating looked steadfastly at cream curves of stone."

Why don't you...?

- Feed the seagulls on O'Connell Bridge.

- Walk on the outside of lampposts just like the eccentric Lamppost Farrell.

- Enjoy a gorgonzola sandwich and a glass of Burgundy in Davy Byrne's, Duke Street.

- Follow Bloom's lunchtime route on *Ulysses The Map* in the centre of the manual.

He said, she said...

"See the animals feed" - Bloom.

Titbit

Joyce loved to be the centre of attention in fine restaurants or at dinners. On one such occasion, F. Scott Fitzgerald who was in awe of Joyce, offered to jump out of the window in his honour.

2.10 pm
Scylla and Charybdis – The one with Shakespeare

Location No 9: Stephen and Bloom in the National Library, Kildare Street

What's the story?

Stephen and the Dublin literary set are hashing out theories about Shakespeare's life, inspirations and work. For the sake of an argument, Stephen claims that Shakespeare is Hamlet's father's ghost. Although he doesn't believe it himself. Bloom comes in on business of his own. Mulligan casts aspersions on Bloom's sexuality.

C'mon!

"Coffined thoughts around me, in mummycases...
Still: but an itch of death is in them."

Why don't you...?

🗨 Act out a scene from Shakespeare.

🗨 Like one of the characters, pepper your conversation with *"don't you know."*

🗨 Visit the National Library and look for the Shakespeare stained-glass window.

He said, she said...

"A father is a necessary evil" - Stephen.

Titbit

Paris in the 1920s was full of Americans fleeing prohibition. *Shakespeare & Co*, who published *Ulysses*, was a book shop, lending library and meeting place for expats. Anyone keen to meet Joyce would go there hoping for an encounter or introduction.

Wandering Rocks - The one with everybody in it

Location No 10: All over Dublin

What's the story?

19 snapshots of people going about their day set against the backdrop of the Viceroy's carriage travelling across the city. The local priest greets everyone. A crumpled flyer floats down the Liffey. While Bloom scours a bookseller's cart in Merchant's Arch for a racy novel for Molly, Blazes Boylan buys treats for her. Ever the scoundrel, he flirts with the shop assistant. Stephen's sisters, impoverished by their father's drinking, scrimp and save. Buck Mulligan enjoys *Damn Bad Cakes*.

"I'll take this one."

Sweets of Sin

"Sweets of Sin... That's a good one."

Why don't you...?

- Search for a racy novel around Merchant's Arch.

- Give everyone the royal wave.

- Have a game of chess.

- Enjoy damn good scones and butter around Dame Street.

He said, she said...

"There's a touch of the artist about old Bloom" - a wandering Dubliner.

Titbit

This chapter has been compared to a game of chess. The Viceroy's carriage represents the wily king, the priest dashes about and everybody else is a pawn.

3.40 pm
Sirens - The one with the sing-song

Location No 11: Bloom in the Ormond Hotel, Ormond Quay

What's the story?

On his way to his rendez-vous with Molly, Blazes Boylan pops into the hotel bar for a quick drink. Bloom secretly follows him in, but doesn't confront him. Inside, Stephen's dad and his cronies enjoy a sing-song. The barmaids, Miss Lydia Douce and Miss Mina Kennedy, keep the boys enthralled by showing a bit of leg and pulling suggestively on the beer pump. The waiter waits while they wait. Bloom tries to hide his fart behind the sound of the tram.

"There's music everywhere."

Why don't you...?

- Smack a garter *"smackwarm against a smackable a woman's warm hosed thigh."*

- Break out into song in a bar on Ormond Quay.

- Go up to the Luas and let rip *"Prrprr. Must be the bur. FFF.OO. Rrpr. Pprrpffrrppfff. Done."*

He said, she said...

"Sure, you'd burst the tympanum of her ear, man, with an organ like yours"
- Stephen's dad.

Titbit

Joyce was a great singer. His wife Nora wished he had chosen singing as a career instead of writing. The opening pages of this chapter sound like an orchestra tuning their instruments before a performance.

5 pm
Cyclops - The one with the fight

Location No 12: Bloom in Barney Kiernan's Pub, Little Britain Street

What's the story?

Bloom goes into the pub on business. The Citizen and his dog Garryowen hold court. Afternoon pints flow freely and talk is full of gossip. Bloom pretends to be oblivious to taunts about his wife and his supposed win on the horses. The barflies think he is too tight-fisted to buy them pints. The Citizen rants about nationalism and targets Bloom for being Jewish. Bloom fights back declaring *"Christ was a jew."* Garryowen and a biscuit tin chase him out of the pub.

"Where is he till I murder him?"

Why don't you...?

- Go for a pint on Capel Street. Sadly, Barney Kiernan's no longer exists.

- Strike up a conversation with the *auld fellas*.

- Curse in Irish, *Póg mo Thóin Ríoga Éireannach!* (Kiss my Royal Irish Arse)

- Try to get a dog to give you the paw.

He said, she said...

"I was blue mouldy for the want of that pint. I could hear it hit the pit of my stomach with a click" - a barfly.

Titbit

Joyce and Ernest Hemingway were drinking buddies. Rumour has it that at the first sign of trouble, Joyce would jump behind him and shout *"Deal with him, Hemingway. Deal with him!"*

Part 3

Evening

"The summer evening had begun to fold the world in its mysterious embrace. The last glow of an all too fleeting day lingered lovingly on sea and strand."

8.25 pm

Nausicaa – The one with the climax

Location No 13: Bloom on Sandymount Strand, Star of the Sea Church

What's the story?

Young Gerty MacDowell, full of romantic whimsy, lingers on the beach with friends minding children. A religious ceremony is taking place in a nearby church. Gerty's fantasies entwine with the eager eye and furtive hand of a dark, mysterious stranger. The prayers become more fervent. Fireworks climax over Sandymount Strand. Who's the man? Bloom! At it again! In his post orgasmic stupor, Bloom reflects on his wife's affair. The clock on the mantelpiece in the priest's house goes cuckoo, cuckoo, cuckoo...

"And then a rocket sprang and bang shot blind and O! then the Roman candle burst and it was like a sigh of O! and everyone cried O!"

Why don't you...?

- Build castles in the sand on Sandymount Strand.

- Answer *"It is half past kissing time"* if somebody asks for the time.

- Have improper thoughts in a public place.

- Check out what Stephen was doing earlier on the Strand in *Proteus*.

He said, she said...

"He was eying her as a snake eyes its prey. Her woman's instinct told her that she had raised the devil in him" - Gerty MacDowell.

Titbit

The bowler, not the cowboy hat, was the most popular hat in the American West. It could be said that it was *"the hat that won the West."* Billy the Kid, Charlie Chaplin, Malcolm McDowell and Liza Minnelli have all worn this iconic hat.

10 pm
Oxen of the Sun – The one with the booze

Location No 14: Bloom and Stephen in Holles Street Hospital

What's the story?

A stampede through the English language from Anglo-Saxon to American slang accompanies a woman giving birth while a gaggle of medical students drink and mouth off. Bloom and Stephen's paths converge as the younger man gets unsteadily inebriated. Our elder hero's paternal instincts are aroused. The men head for the pub for more *bluggy drunkables* as language swills in the bottom of a pint glass.

"Hoopsa boyaboy hoopsa!"

waaagh!

Why don't you...?

- Enjoy a variety of drinks in a nearby pub.

- Speak in *ye olde English*.

- Feign a womanish simper and immodest squirming of your body.

He said, she said...

"We are all born in the same way but we all die in different ways" - Bloom.

Titbit

Joyce threw every literary technique and style at this book. He made up his own words and drove the editors of the *Oxford English Dictionary* mad. The average newspaper uses 500 different words. *Ulysses* has over 30,000.

Part 4

Night-time

"Snakes of river fog creep slowly. From drains, clefts, cesspools, middens arise on all sides stagnant fumes."

11.25 pm
Circe – The one in the brothel

Location No 15: Bloom and Stephen in Monto (around James Joyce Street)

What's the story?

A surreal meander through Monto, Dublin's red light district. Bloom searches for Stephen. He has visions of people changing costume and shape before his eyes. Midsummer madness! Bloom is put on trial. Decomposing Paddy Dignam comes to his defence. Bloom is declared pregnant and then crowned King of Ireland. He finds Stephen in a brothel. Bella Cohen, a madam, dominates Bloom. Stephen fights the ghost of his mother and a British soldier. Having faced their demons, they leave Monto.

"Exuberant female. Enormously I desiderate your domination."

Why don't you...?

🍂 Hold your testicles (or somebody else's) and proclaim yourself King of Ireland.

🍂 Re-enact grotesque parodies of what has happened to you during the day.

🍂 Sing *"I gave it to Molly, because she was jolly, the leg of a duck, the leg of a duck."*

He said, she said...

"Has little mousey any tickles tonight?" - a young whore.

Titbit

In 1904 Monto was Europe's largest red light district. Joyce named it Nighttown which was slang among Dublin journalists for the late shift on a newspaper. Rumour has it, the then Prince of Wales (later King Edward VII) lost his virginity there.

12.40 am

Eumaeus – The one with the seaman

Location No 16: Bloom and Stephen in a cabman's shelter near Butt Bridge

What's the story?

Bloom and Stephen are knackered after a long day. Bloom ridiculously sober. Stephen disgracefully drunk. They have dodgy coffee and stale buns. Their conversation is disjointed and directionless. Paralysis oozes out of the floor boards. An old sailor weaves tall tales. He pisses loudly in the gutter. A horse takes a big shit to close the episode.

"Buffalo Bill shoots to kill,

Why don't you...?

- Drink cold coffee and eat dodgy buns.

- Pick a target, take aim and fire!

- Tell stories for hours on end.

He said, she said...

"Every country, they say, our own distressful included, has the government it deserves" - Bloom.

Titbit

Bodily functions and fluids obsessed Joyce - his *arsethetic* vision. H.G. Wells wrote to him *"you really believe in chastity, purity and the personal God and that is why you are always breaking out into cries of c*nt, sh*t and hell."*

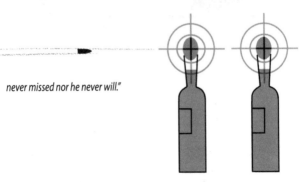

never missed nor he never will."

1 am

Ithaca – The one under the stars

Location No 17: Bloom and Stephen in No 7 Eccles Street

What's the story?

The kettle boiled. They talk. They don't talk. They drink. They take a pee under the stars. Bloom offers Stephen the couch. He declines. Stephen disappears into the night. Bloom potters around the kitchen. He clambers into bed with Molly, wiping up another man's potted meat crumbs from the sheets. He kisses her rump. He is home. He drifts off... to... sleep.

"The heaventree of stars hung with humid nightblue fruit."

Why don't you...?

- Gaze at the stars while taking a piss, seeing how grand a trajectory you can create.

- Drink cocoa.

- Kiss somebody on the cheek.

He said, she said...

"Kiss the plump mellow yellow smellow melons of a rump" - Bloom.

Titbit

Joyce often wrote in bed with domestic chaos all around him. Nora complained that he kept her awake all night, chuckling to himself while composing *Ulysses*.

2 am

Penelope – The one with Herself

Location No 18: Molly and Bloom in bed top to tail

What's the story?

Awake in the middle of the night, Molly's mind as well as her hands, travel everywhere. The tarot cards have promised her an encounter with a stranger. She and Bloom haven't had sex in years. She fantasises about doing it with a priest. She smiles over Bloom's lovable idiosyncrasies. She farts. Dreams up filthy words she'd use to spice up her love making. She recalls the day that Leopold proposed to her on Howth Head. She said YES!

"I put my arms around him yes and drew him down to me so he could feel my breasts all perfume yes and his heart was going like mad and yes I said yes I will Yes."

Get a room!

Why don't you...?

- Sleep top to tail.

- Get a tarot card reading.

- Take a day trip to Howth Head.

- Say YES!

She said...

"I wouldn't give a snap of my two fingers for all their learning why don't they go and create something" - Molly Bloom.

Titbit

The sound of a woman's authentic voice was shocking to some of Joyce's contemporaries. He was always documenting Nora's phrases and comments on his shirt cuffs. Perhaps most of this chapter comes from her rather than him.

"Most beautiful book come out of Ireland in my time"
Buck Mulligan.

"Love, life, voyage round your own little world"
Leopold Bloom.

"The eternal affirmation of the spirit of man in literature"
Stephen Dedalus.

"Racier than one of mine"
Paul de Kock.

Further Information

For further information visit www.atitagain.ie

Thanks to

Chuffey Media, Ciara Laverty, Dublin UNESCO City of Literature, Edwina Keown, Emma Harding, Failte Ireland, Liam Birkett, James Joyce Centre, Sweny's Chemist, William Barton and the Waiter who waits while you wait.

End Note

If you fancy yourself as a Joycean scholar and spot any errata, we'd be deeliarred to hear from you.

Notes